WARRIORS

A SHADOW IN
RIVERCLAN

WARRIORS

A SHADOW IN RIVERCLAN

CREATED BY
ERIN HUNTER

WRITTEN BY
DAN JOLLEY

ART BY
JAMES L. BARRY

An Imprint of HarperCollinsPublishers

WARRIORS

GRAPHIC NOVELS

Warriors: A Shadow in RiverClan
Created by Erin Hunter
Written by Dan Jolley
Art by James L. Barry

HarperAlley is an imprint of HarperCollins Publishers.

Text copyright © 2020 by Working Partners Limited
Art copyright © 2020 by HarperCollins Publishers
All rights reserved. Manufactured in China.

978-0-06-294665-2 (hardcover) — ISBN 978-0-06-294664-5 (pbk)

20 21 22 23 24   SCP   10 9 8 7 6 5 4 3 2 1
❖
First Edition

HOME...

EVERY CAT KNOWS WHERE THEIR HOME IS, DON'T THEY?

OR AT LEAST WHERE THEY BELONG.

EVERY CAT...EXCEPT ME.

THIS IS RIVERCLAN.

IT'S SUPPOSED TO BE MY HOME.

THEY HAVE TRAINED HARD TO UNDERSTAND THE WAYS OF YOUR NOBLE CODE, AND I COMMEND THEM TO YOU AS WARRIORS IN THEIR TURN.

I, LEOPARDSTAR, LEADER OF RIVERCLAN, CALL MY ANCESTORS TO LOOK DOWN ON THESE APPRENTICES.

FEATHERPAW, DO YOU PROMISE TO UPHOLD THE WARRIOR CODE AND PROTECT AND DEFEND YOUR CLAN...

...EVEN AT THE COST OF YOUR LIFE?

LEOPARDSTAR'S WORDS RING IN MY EARS...

ECHOING DOWN THE LONG, PAINFUL ROAD THAT HAS LED ME TO THIS PLACE.

AND NOW...HERE WE ARE. ABOUT TO BE NAMED WARRIORS OF RIVERCLAN. SO WHY IS THE QUESTION GNAWING AT ME –

AM I READY?

I KNOW WHAT GRAYSTRIPE WOULD SAY. "MAKE YOUR CLAN PROUD."

SO...

I DO.

THEN BY THE POWERS OF STARCLAN, I GIVE YOU YOUR WARRIOR NAME.

FEATHERPAW, FROM THIS MOMENT ON, YOU WILL BE KNOWN AS FEATHERTAIL.

STARCLAN HONORS YOUR BRAVERY AND COMPASSION...

...AND WE WELCOME YOU AS A FULL WARRIOR OF RIVERCLAN!

STORMPAW, DO YOU PROMISE TO UPHOLD THE WARRIOR CODE AND PROTECT AND DEFEND YOUR CLAN...

I BARELY EVEN HEAR THE REST OF LEOPARDSTAR'S WORDS.

STORMPAW, FROM THIS MOMENT ON, YOU WILL BE KNOWN AS STORMFUR.

STARCLAN HONORS YOUR STRENGTH AND LOYALTY...

MY BROTHER'S HAPPINESS MAKES ME HAPPY. AT LEAST A LITTLE. I KNOW HE DOESN'T HAVE MY DOUBTS.

THE DOUBTS THAT WILL NOT GO AWAY.

...AND WE WELCOME YOU AS A FULL WARRIOR OF RIVERCLAN!

THIS IS SUPPOSED TO BE ONE OF THE PROUDEST DAYS OF A CAT'S LIFE.

FEATHERTAIL. STORMFUR.

FEATHERTAIL. STORMFUR.

SO WHY CAN'T I TAKE ANY PRIDE IN IT? ANY JOY?

WHY DOES EVERYTHING HAVE TO BE CAST IN SHADOW?

THIS IS SUCH A GREAT EVENING! I'M SO HAPPY FOR YOU!

YES...YES, IT'S A GREAT NIGHT.

NOW THAT THE OFFICIAL STUFF IS OUT OF THE WAY...

I CANNOT TELL YOU HOW PROUD OF YOU I AM RIGHT NOW, FEATHERP—

OH, EXCUSE ME. FEATHERTAIL.

YOU'RE GOING TO BE A GREAT WARRIOR!

AND YOU. LITTLE STORMKIT, ALL GROWN UP!

MY BROTHER WOULD BE SO THRILLED TO SEE YOU TODAY.

STONEFUR.

I MISS HIM.

AN ENTIRE NIGHT SPENT IN SILENCE. IT WON'T BOTHER ME...

...THOUGH I'M AFRAID NOT BEING ABLE TO TALK MIGHT KILL MY BROTHER.

I DON'T KNOW ABOUT COMMUNING WITH STARCLAN... BUT THIS CERTAINLY DOES GIVE ME PLENTY OF TIME FOR MEMORIES.

MISTYFOOT AND STONEFUR WERE THE BEST MENTORS WE COULD HAVE ASKED FOR.

THEY WORKED HARD TRAINING STORMPAW AND ME. TAUGHT US TO FIGHT AND HUNT AND SWIM AND FISH.

THOSE ARE THE GOOD MEMORIES.

MOST OF THE REST OF THEM...

ARE JUST PAINFUL NOW.

TIGERSTAR SAID SHADOWCLAN AND RIVERCLAN SHOULD JOIN TOGETHER. BECOME ONE CLAN.

AND LEOPARDSTAR AGREED.

SHE THOUGHT IT WOULD MAKE RIVERCLAN STRONGER...ALLYING WITH ANOTHER POWERFUL CLAN.

SHE WAS WRONG.

TIGERSTAR TOOK ALL THE POWER FOR HIMSELF.

SLASH

WE WOULD'VE DIED THAT NIGHT, TOO. STORMFUR AND ME.

IT FELT LIKE WE ALREADY HAD.

BUT OUR FATHER CAME FOR US.

HE TOOK US TO THUNDERCLAN, ALONG WITH MISTYFOOT. HE SAVED ALL OUR LIVES.

SO WE LEFT OUR HOME... AND STONEFUR...BEHIND US.

BUT I SHOULD'VE KNOWN THAT TIME OF PEACE COULDN'T LAST.

IT ENDED THE DAY LEOPARDSTAR WALKED INTO THE THUNDERCLAN CAMP.

NOW THAT TIGERSTAR AND SCOURGE WERE BOTH DEAD, SHE SAID, THERE WAS NO MORE TIGERCLAN.

RIVERCLAN WAS RE-FORMING.

COME BACK TO RIVERCLAN. IT'LL BE THE WAY IT WAS BEFORE.

SHE OFFERED TO MAKE MISTYFOOT HER NEW DEPUTY.

TO GIVE US ALL A CHANCE TO "HELP REBUILD THE CLAN."

I GUESS MISTYFOOT THOUGHT IT WAS TOO GOOD AN OFFER TO TURN DOWN.

"HELP REBUILD THE CLAN."

SO HERE I AM. I'VE SWORN THE OATH. TAKEN MY WARRIOR NAME. LIKE IT OR NOT, I'M A RIVERCLAN CAT AGAIN.

BUT HOW? HOW CAN I BE THE LOYAL WARRIOR MY CLAN NEEDS, WHEN I DON'T TRUST LEOPARDSTAR AT ALL?

THAT'S IT! THE SUN'S UP, THE VIGIL'S OVER! WE DID IT!

WE'RE WARRIORS! REAL WARRIORS!

STORMFUR... DO YOU EVER THINK MAYBE...

DO YOU EVER WONDER IF WE MADE THE RIGHT CHOICE?

RIGHT CHOICE? WHAT'RE YOU TALKING ABOUT?

DO YOU EVER WONDER IF WE SHOULD'VE STAYED IN THUNDERCLAN, IS WHAT I'M TALKING ABOUT. WITH GRAYSTRIPE.

NO CAT EVER TRIED TO KILL US THERE.

IT WASN'T HOME, EXACTLY, BUT IT WAS SAFE.

ARE YOU SERIOUS?

IT'S A LITTLE LATE TO BE HAVING THOUGHTS LIKE THAT, DON'T YOU THINK?

...

YEAH. I SUPPOSE IT IS.

THERE ARE OUR NEW WARRIORS! CONGRATULATIONS!

GOT THROUGH YOUR VIGIL ALL RIGHT, I SEE!

THANKS! IT WAS NO PROBLEM!

YES, THANK YOU.

LOOK, WHATEVER HAPPENS, I KNOW I'M A RIVERCLAN CAT. AND I THINK YOU KNOW YOU ARE, TOO.

WE CAN GET PAST WHAT HAPPENED BEFORE.

I'LL BE THE BEST RIVERCLAN WARRIOR I CAN BE.

I DON'T SAY IT OUT LOUD, BUT THE WORDS ARE RIGHT THERE ON MY TONGUE: "IF THEY'LL LET ME."

AND I DO TRY MY BEST, AS NEWLEAF TURNS THE LAND GREEN AGAIN.

I PUT THE TRAINING MISTYFOOT GAVE US TO GOOD USE.

SPLISH

THERE WE GO –

SPLASH

THWACK!

NO, THANKS.

OH...OKAY...

SOME DAYS IT FEELS LIKE MY BRAIN HAS BECOME A SWARM OF BEES INSIDE MY HEAD.

HOW CAN I LIVE WITH THE CATS WHO WANTED MY BROTHER AND ME DEAD JUST BECAUSE OF WHO OUR PARENTS WERE?

WHO CHEERED WHEN STONEFUR DIED?

HOW CAN I EVER LOOK AT LEOPARDSTAR AND SEE ANYTHING...

...OTHER THAN HER GIVING THAT ORDER?

THE DISTANCE STARTS SMALL...

...BUT IT GROWS EVERY DAY.

FEATHERTAIL!

THE FISH ARE JUMPING UP HERE! WANT TO JOIN US?

NO, THANKS.

I'M FINE WHERE I AM.

PART OF ME WANTS TO TELL MYSELF THAT I'M FINE WITH IT. THAT I DON'T NEED ANY OTHER CAT.

AT THE SAME TIME, I SEE HOW WELL STORMFUR HAS FIT IN.

AND I WONDER HOW TERRIBLE A SISTER I AM THAT I FEEL JEALOUS.

LISTEN, FEATHERTAIL. I KNOW YOU'RE HAVING TROUBLE, AND I WANT TO HELP. I REALLY DO.

BUT I'VE MADE MY CHOICE. I HOPE YOU CAN UNDERSTAND THAT. I NEED TO BE PART OF RIVERCLAN.

AND THAT MEANS... WELL, IT MEANS FORGIVING THE CATS WHO HURT US.

HE WANTS A RESPONSE FROM ME. HE DESERVES ONE. BUT I CAN ONLY GIVE HIM SILENCE.

SO WHY DOES IT FEEL SO ROTTEN?

SNFF SNFF

JUST ACROSS THAT RIVER LIES THUNDERCLAN TERRITORY.

I CAN'T HELP WONDERING HOW GRAYSTRIPE IS DOING.

IS HE HEALTHY? DOES HE MISS US? WILL HE—

SQUEEEK!

WHY IS A THUNDERCLAN CAT SITTING HERE ON RIVERCLAN TERRITORY, FEATHERTAIL?

AND WHY IN THE NAME OF STARCLAN WOULD YOU GIVE AWAY FRESH-KILL?

IT'S FINE, REALLY, YOU CAN KEEP IT –

I DON'T WANT TO FIGHT ABOUT IT....

FERNCLOUD WAS ALREADY CHASING THE SQUIRREL WHEN IT CROSSED THE RIVER.

IT BELONGED TO HER.

RIDICULOUS!

PREY GOES WHERE IT WANTS. IF FERNCLOUD WERE A DECENT HUNTER, SHE WOULD'VE CAUGHT IT IN HER OWN TERRITORY.

AND ON TOP OF THAT... HOW DARE YOU UNSHEATHE YOUR CLAWS AT YOUR CLANMATES?

ESPECIALLY IN DEFENSE OF A CAT FROM ANOTHER CLAN?

I NEED TO KNOW WHAT'S IN YOUR HEART, FEATHERTAIL. YOU'RE GOING TO HAVE TO PROVE YOUR LOYALTY.

IT'S ALL I CAN DO NOT TO LAUGH IN HER FACE.

I'M THE ONE WHO NEEDS TO PROVE MY LOYALTY?

SHE'S THE ONE WHO BETRAYED RIVERCLAN!

SHE'S THE ONE WHO THREW IN WITH TIGERSTAR!

WE'RE JUST SUPPOSED TO FORGET THAT?

WELL, I HAVEN'T FORGOTTEN.

THIS IS HUMILIATING.

MORE SO AS EACH DAY DRAGS BY.

BUT AT LEAST IT GIVES ME AN EXCUSE NOT TO TALK TO ANY CAT.

THAT'S A GOOD LOOK FOR YOU, FEATHERTAIL!

YOU KNOW, THIS PUNISHMENT THING HAS WORKED OUT WELL FOR THE CLAN.

WE'RE A LITTLE SHORT ON YOUNG CATS, AFTER ALL. IT'S NICE TO HAVE SOME CAT TO DO THE APPRENTICE WORK.

HOW WOULD YOU LIKE TO EAT THIS MOSS?

HEY, EASY NOW, IT'S ONLY FOR ANOTHER COUPLE OF DAYS.

IT WOULDN'T BE SO BAD IF SOME OF THE OTHER WARRIORS WEREN'T SO FILTHY.

I THINK BLACKCLAW TEARS UP HIS NEST MOSS ON PURPOSE. HE'S TRYING TO MAKE THIS AS HARD FOR ME AS POSSIBLE.

WELL...YOU REALIZE... SOME OF THE OTHER WARRIORS ARE PRETTY ANGRY WITH YOU.

AND, HONESTLY, THEY HAVE A RIGHT TO BE.

YOU'RE TAKING THEIR SIDE?

I'M NOT TELLING YOU ANYTHING YOU DON'T ALREADY KNOW.

GIVING AWAY PREY? YOU TOOK SOMETHING RIVERCLAN NEEDED. IF WE START LETTING OTHER CATS HUNT ON OUR TERRITORY...

WELL, THEN WHO'S GOING TO RESPECT OUR BORDERS AT ALL? THE WHOLE CLAN WOULD SUFFER.

HONESTLY... THE TRUTH IS...

I DO STILL FEEL LOYALTY TO THUNDERCLAN. AND NOT JUST BECAUSE OUR FATHER IS DEPUTY THERE.

IT JUST SEEMED NATURAL TO HELP FERNCLOUD.

STORMFUR, THUNDERCLAN TOOK US IN WHEN RIVERCLAN TURNED AGAINST US.

WE BOTH TRAINED AS APPRENTICES ALONGSIDE FERNCLOUD!

WE ALL FOUGHT BLOODCLAN TOGETHER. ALL THE THUNDERCLAN APPRENTICES.

I KNOW. I KNOW WHAT YOU'RE SAYING IS TRUE. IT'S JUST... IT DOESN'T CHANGE ANYTHING.

MAYBE NOT. BUT I KNOW FERNCLOUD BETTER THAN I DO MOST OF THE CATS HERE.

THAT PREY DID BELONG TO HER.

AND I COULDN'T LET THE OTHER CATS HURT HER. I JUST COULDN'T.

YOU'VE GOT TO MAKE UP YOUR MIND, FEATHERTAIL.

A CAT CAN'T STAND WITH HER PAWS IN MORE THAN ONE CLAN.

AT LEAST THAT WAS THE LAST OF THE NEST MOSS FOR THE DAY.

HEY, LISTEN – THERE'S A NICE MINNOW ON THE FRESH-KILL PILE.

WANT TO SHARE IT WITH ME?

I'D BE HONORED.

LEOPARDSTAR!

WHAT'S WRONG, BLACKCLAW?

PATROL JUST PICKED UP A SCENT — A STRONG ONE.

ROGUE CATS, INSIDE THE RIVERCLAN BORDER.

ALL RIGHT.

I'LL TAKE A FRESH PATROL AND SCARE THEM OFF.

FEATHERTAIL. STORMFUR.

COME WITH ME.

IT WAS OVER THIS WAY...

SNFF SNFF

STRANGERS! THIS IS RIVERCLAN TERRITORY!

YOU NEED TO LEAVE –

LOOK HOW SKINNY THEY ARE! BLACKCLAW COULD'VE CHASED THEM OFF BY HIMSELF.

WHAT WARRIOR NEEDS A WHOLE PATROL TO DEAL WITH THESE THREE?

THOSE POOR LITTLE MITES!

THEY'RE TERRIFIED.

WHY ARE YOU HERE?

WHAT BUSINESS DO YOU HAVE WITH RIVERCLAN?

MY NAME IS SASHA. THESE ARE MY KITS... HAWK AND MOTH.

PLEASE. WE ASK ONLY FOR YOUR MERCY.

PLEASE LET US JOIN RIVERCLAN.

IS SHE SERIOUS? THERE'S NO WAY!

ALL THEY WANT TO DO IS TAKE ADVANTAGE OF US!

STARCLAN, WHAT A BULLY BLACKCLAW IS.

LEOPARDSTAR... WE CAN'T JUST TURN THEM AWAY.

PLEASE... LEOPARDSTAR?

PLEASE. WE'LL WORK HARD. I SWEAR.

I'VE... I'VE ALREADY LOST ONE KIT. I DON'T WANT TO LOSE THESE TWO.

FOR WHAT IT'S WORTH... I WAS JUST TELLING FEATHERTAIL THAT WE COULD USE SOME NEW APPRENTICES.

THE NURSERY'S NEARLY EMPTY.

HMMM.

YOUR KITS DO LOOK HEALTHY. OR THEY WOULD, IF THEY HAD A FEW SOLID MEALS.

ALMOST READY TO BE APPRENTICED.

FINE.

"...COME WITH US."

ADMIT IT. YOU'LL ENJOY HAVING SOME NEW APPRENTICES AROUND TO DO THE CAMP WORK, RIGHT?

IN CASE YOU GET IN TROUBLE AGAIN?

QUIET, YOU.

IT TAKES BARELY A QUARTER-MOON
FOR SASHA TO FIT RIGHT IN WITH RIVERCLAN.

SHE PROVES TO BE A CAPABLE
ENOUGH HUNTER...

AND THOUGH SHE HASN'T YET TAKEN A WARRIOR'S NAME, THE OTHER WARRIORS SEEM TO ACCEPT HER READILY ENOUGH.

LITTLE WONDER. SHE'S CHARMING. OUTGOING. EVERY CAT ENJOYS HER COMPANY.

PART OF ME WONDERS WHAT THAT FEELS LIKE.

I SHOULDN'T WONDER. NOT WHEN I'VE WORKED SO HARD TO PUSH EVERY CAT AWAY.

STILL. IT'S JUST... IT'S NOT FAIR. SASHA WASN'T BORN INTO ANY CLAN.

WHY SHOULD SHE BE ACCEPTED, WHEN I NEVER WILL BE?

OH!

FEATHERTAIL.

WHAT DO YOU THINK OF OUR NEWEST CAT? IS SHE FITTING IN WELL?

I...WOULD SAY SO, YES.

THOUGH SHE SEEMS HESITANT ABOUT TAKING A WARRIOR'S NAME.

YES. SHE'S TOLD ME SHE NEEDS A BIT OF TIME TO THINK ABOUT IT.

I RESPECT THAT.

AFTER ALL...

JOINING A CLAN IS NOT SOMETHING TO BE TAKEN LIGHTLY. YOU UNDERSTAND THAT BETTER THAN MOST, DON'T YOU?

OH, I UNDERSTAND, LEOPARDSTAR. BETTER THAN YOU DO.

SASHA'S KITS — HAWK AND MOTH — SETTLE INTO CLAN LIFE JUST AS EASILY AS THEIR MOTHER.

IT SEEMS AS IF THEY'VE BEEN PART OF RIVERCLAN FOREVER.

I HOPE BEING HUNGRY IS THE WORST THING THAT EVER HAPPENS TO THEM.

I HOPE THEY NEVER HAVE TO FACE THE TERROR THAT STORMFUR AND I DID.

LOOK AT THOSE TWO. A ROCK COULD PAY BETTER ATTENTION TO THE KITS.

BUT *I* AM PAYING ATTENTION... AND IT ONLY TAKES A HEARTBEAT TO REMIND ME –

HAWK AND MOTH ARE FITTING IN WELL, BUT THEY WEREN'T BORN HERE...

AND THEY DON'T KNOW THE RIVER!

SASHA!

HAWK ALMOST DROWNED. HE GOT IN THE WATER AND WASHED AWAY!

AAAAAHHH!

HAWK!

FEATHERTAIL, THAT...

THAT WAS BEAUTIFUL.

YOU REACTED THE WAY A TRUE WARRIOR WOULD. THAT KIT'S ALIVE NOW BECAUSE OF YOUR ACTIONS.

YES, WELL.

I DIDN'T DO IT FOR YOU.

IT TAKES A WHILE FOR MY LEGS TO STOP SHAKING.

NOT THAT I WOULD LET ANY CAT SEE THEM SHAKE.

FEATHERTAIL...?

I, UH... I'D LIKE TO TALK TO YOU...

IF YOU DON'T MIND?

IF YOU DO MIND, THAT'S FINE, I DON'T WANT TO DISTURB YOU. IT CAN WAIT....

I JUST WANTED TO... TO THANK YOU... FOR SAVING HAWK.

HE AND MOTH WERE SO SCARED BECAUSE... WELL, THEIR BROTHER, TADPOLE...

TADPOLE DROWNED. EARLIER THIS NEWLEAF. THEY BOTH...

IT, UM, HAPPENED IN FRONT OF THEM. THEY BOTH SAW IT.

ANYWAY.

I JUST WANTED TO SAY THANKS.

SASHA. WAIT.

WOULD YOU LIKE TO SHARE SOME PREY?

WE'VE BEEN WANDERING. SINCE TADPOLE DIED.

JUST TRYING TO SURVIVE.

NOT VERY WELL, AS YOU SAW YOU WHEN YOU FOUND US.

WE TRIED TO JOIN A GROUP OF BARN CATS, BUT THAT TURNED OUT TO BE... NOT SUCH A GOOD PLACE.

SO WE HAD TO LEAVE.

ALL I WANT IS A TRUE HOME FOR MY KITS. YOU KNOW?

I HOPED RIVERCLAN COULD BE THAT HOME.

AND, SO FAR, IT HAS BEEN. I CAN'T TELL YOU HOW GRATEFUL I AM. WE ALL ARE.

WHAT HAPPENED TO THE KITS' FATHER?

IS HE STILL AROUND?

N-NO...

NO, HE DIED.

AND JUST LIKE THAT — SASHA AND I BECAME NEARLY INSEPARABLE.

NO ONE IS AS SURPRISED AS I AM THAT SASHA AND I HAVE BECOME FRIENDS.

MAYBE THIS IS THE ONLY WAY I COULD HAVE A FRIEND.

LIKE THIS?

SPLASH

TWO OUTCASTS. DRAWN TOGETHER.

WITH SASHA'S BLESSING, I EVEN START TEACHING HAWK AND MOTH HOW TO SWIM.

NOW, YOUR MENTORS, WHOEVER THEY'RE GOING TO BE, WILL SHOW YOU TO REALLY SWIM. LIKE THE REST OF RIVERCLAN.

BUT THERE'S NO HARM IN LEARNING THE BASICS. THIS WAY YOU'LL BE SAFE, CLOSE TO THE RIVER.

BUT YOU SHOULD STILL NEVER SWIM ALONE. NOT UNTIL YOUR MENTORS HAVE TOLD YOU IT'S ALL RIGHT.

SAY THANK YOU!

THANK YOU, FEATHERTAIL!

THANKS, FEATHERTAIL!

AS I WATCH THE KITS SPLASH AROUND IN THE SHALLOWS, I REALIZE I'M FEELING SOMETHING I HAVEN'T FELT BEFORE.

SOMETHING DEEP INSIDE ME. IN MY HEART.

IS THIS WHAT BEING PART OF A CLAN IS SUPPOSED TO FEEL LIKE?

I HAVE TO SAY, FEATHERTAIL, IT'S GOOD TO SEE YOU MAKING FRIENDS. I WASN'T SURE THAT WAS GOING TO HAPPEN HERE.

NEITHER WAS I.

AND YOU KNOW WHAT WOULD BE EVEN BETTER...IS IF I COULD MENTOR ONE OF THOSE KITS. HAWK IS VERY BRAVE, AND MOTH IS SO CLEVER!

I THINK I COULD TEACH THEM A LOT.... PLUS, I THINK I CAN TRUST SASHA. SINCE SHE HAD NOTHING TO DO WITH... EVERYTHING THAT HAPPENED.

AND, YOU KNOW.

IT IS NICE TO HAVE A FRIEND OTHER THAN YOU.

HEY!

THAT'S HORRIBLE!

AND I THOUGHT MY KITS WOULD BE SAFE HERE....

I THINK THEY WILL BE. DON'T WORRY. RIVERCLAN ISN'T LIKE THAT ANYMORE.

ARE YOU SURE?

THAT SIMPLE QUESTION TAKES ME OFFGUARD. AM I SURE? HAS RIVERCLAN CHANGED?

AND IT HITS ME. YES. THE CLAN HAS CHANGED. THEY'VE ALL LEARNED FROM THEIR MISTAKES.

I CAN'T IMAGINE THEM FOLLOWING A LEADER LIKE TIGERSTAR NOW.

OR DOING KITS OR APPRENTICES HARM FOR NO REAL REASON.

I'M SURE. YES.

BESIDES... I'LL BE LOOKING OUT FOR YOUR KITS. AND SO WILL STORMFUR AND MISTYFOOT.

THANK YOU.

AND...I HOPE YOU CAN LEARN TO TRUST YOUR CLAN AGAIN. I KNOW CATS MAKE MISTAKES...

THE ONES WHO LISTENED TO TIGERSTAR SHOULDN'T BE BLAMED FOREVER, SHOULD THEY?

NOT IF THEY'VE LEARNED BETTER NOW.

NEWLEAF COMES AND GOES.

GREENLEAF HAS BEGUN BY THE TIME LEOPARDSTAR CALLS RIVERCLAN TOGETHER AGAIN.

I, LEOPARDSTAR, LEADER OF RIVERCLAN, CALL MY ANCESTORS TO LOOK DOWN ON THESE KITS.

TONIGHT'S THE NIGHT. HAWK AND MOTH BECOME HAWKPAW AND MOTHPAW. OFFICIALLY RIVERCLAN APPRENTICES.

TONIGHT LEOPARDSTAR PICKS THEIR MENTORS.

MOTH AND HAWK, YOU HAVE REACHED THE AGE OF SIX MOONS, AND IT IS TIME FOR YOU TO BE APPRENTICED.

FROM THIS DAY ON, UNTIL YOU RECEIVE YOUR WARRIOR NAMES...

YOU WILL BE KNOWN AS MOTHPAW AND HAWKPAW.

MOTHPAW, YOUR MENTOR WILL BE MISTYFOOT. I HOPE THAT SHE WILL PASS ON ALL SHE KNOWS TO YOU.

MISTYFOOT, COME FORWARD.

MISTYFOOT, YOU ARE A FINE DEPUTY FOR RIVERCLAN AND TAUGHT FEATHERTAIL WELL WHEN YOU WERE HER MENTOR.

YOU WILL BE MOTHPAW'S MENTOR...

AND I EXPECT YOU TO PASS ON ALL YOUR KNOWLEDGE TO HER.

AND I...

HAWKPAW!
MOTHPAW!

HAWKPAW!
MOTHPAW!

I SHOULD BE HAPPY
FOR THE KITS.

MISTYFOOT WAS A GREAT
MENTOR, AND HAS ALWAYS BEEN
A LOYAL CAT.

I TRUST HER WITH MOTHPAW.

LEOPARDSTAR, THOUGH...

HOW CAN I EVER
TRUST HER?

ALTHOUGH...SHE LOOKS AS IF SHE
WANTS TO DO HER BEST WITH HIM.
MAKE HIM A GREAT WARRIOR.

STARCLAN, I HOPE
THAT'S TRUE.

THIS IS EVERYTHING I'VE EVER WANTED FOR MY KITS!

THEY'LL HAVE A WHOLE CLAN OF CATS TO LOOK OUT FOR THEM HERE. THEY'LL BELONG!

THE LIFE OF A ROGUE CAT IS SO HARD...AND NOW THEY WON'T EVER HAVE TO FACE IT.

EXCEPT — WHAT YOU WERE SAYING, BEFORE...

WILL HAWKPAW BE SAFE WITH LEOPARDSTAR?

I WISH YOU COULD HAVE BEEN HIS MENTOR INSTEAD. I KNOW YOU'D TAKE CARE OF HIM.

I WISH I COULD'VE BEEN HAWKPAW'S MENTOR, TOO. BUT THIS IS A GOOD THING.

IT'S UNUSUAL, AND A REAL HONOR, FOR THE CLAN'S LEADER TO TAKE AN APPRENTICE.

SEE, BY MAKING HERSELF AND THE CLAN DEPUTY HAWKPAW AND MOTHPAW'S MENTORS...

...SHE'S TELLING THE CLAN THAT THE TWO APPRENTICES BELONG, EVEN THOUGH THEY WEREN'T BORN IN RIVERCLAN.

THAT WOULD NEVER HAVE HAPPENED UNDER TIGERSTAR.

AM I LYING TO HER?

HAS LEOPARDSTAR CHANGED ENOUGH THAT SHE WANTS TO PROTECT THE OUTSIDERS SHE'S LET JOIN RIVERCLAN?

I THINK I'D BETTER KEEP AN EYE ON MOTHPAW AND HAWKPAW.

JUST IN CASE.

SASHA'S STILL DOING WELL. SOME OF HER CHARM EVEN RUBS OFF ON ME, IF ONLY A TINY BIT.

IT WAS TRUE, WHAT I SAID TO STORMFUR. IT IS NICE TO HAVE FRIENDS.

NICE TO BE PART OF A CLAN. FULLY PART OF IT.

I THINK I'VE MISSED THIS.

DID YOU SEE HOW HIGH THAT RABBIT JUMPED?

LIKE IT HAD WINGS ALL OF A SUDDEN!

WINGS OR NOT, I WAS RIGHT THERE WHEN IT CAME BACK DOWN.

HA! YEAH YOU WERE!

I'LL GET YOU!

NUH-UH, YOU'LL NEVER CATCH ME!

GOTCHA!

OOF!

OW!

HEY! NOT SO ROUGH!

YOU KNOW WHAT HAPPENS TO BAD LITTLE KITS, DON'T YOU?

TIGERSTAR COMES AND GETS THEM!

SORRY! SORRY! I'LL BE GOOD! SORRY!

SASHA...

I NEED TO ASK YOU SOMETHING.

WHEN MOSSPELT MENTIONED TIGERSTAR... WHY DID YOU LOOK SO UPSET?

TIGERSTAR'S DEAD. ALL HIS CRIMES ARE IN THE PAST. HE'S GOT NOTHING TO DO WITH YOU.

IT'S JUST... IT'S HARD TO HEAR HIS NAME USED LIKE THAT.

TO FRIGHTEN KITS.

NO MATTER WHAT HE DID.

BUT...WHY?

YOU DIDN'T EVEN KNOW TIGERSTAR!

I NEVER SAID THAT.

PARDON ME?

WHAT EXACTLY ARE YOU SAYING?

I...

FEATHERTAIL, I DID KNOW TIGERSTAR.

I KNEW HIM VERY WELL.

TIGERSTAR NEVER MET HIS KITS. HE NEVER EVEN KNEW I WAS EXPECTING!

PLEASE DON'T PUNISH THEM FOR WHAT HE DID WRONG. THAT'S... THAT'S WHAT HE TRIED TO DO TO YOU, ISN'T IT?

HURT YOU BECAUSE OF WHO YOUR PARENTS WERE?

PLEASE. FEATHERTAIL. WE'RE FRIENDS, AREN'T WE?

WHAT SHE'S DONE IS INEXCUSABLE. THE CLAN WOULD BE JUSTIFIED TO CAST THEM OUT. MAKE THEM ROGUES AGAIN.

BUT IT ONLY TAKES A HEARTBEAT FOR ME TO KNOW I CAN'T DO THAT TO THEM.

SASHA'S RIGHT. IT'S NOT THEIR FAULT.

BEFORE, I KEPT AN EYE ON HAWKPAW AND MOTHPAW TO MAKE SURE LEOPARDSTAR DIDN'T HURT THEM.

NOW...

SASHA'S HORRIBLE SECRET POUNDS IN MY HEAD. LETS ME SEE THE TRUTH.

NOW IT FEELS AS IF I HAVE TO KEEP AN EYE ON EVERY CAT.

AND THE TRUTH IS...

I CAN'T TRUST ANY CAT.

IT'S BETTER TO BE ALONE.

AT LEAST I CAN TRUST MYSELF.

STORMFUR HAS ALWAYS BEEN TRUE TO ME. ALWAYS THE ONE FRIEND I KNEW I HAD.

BUT THIS IS TOO BIG TO PUT ON HIM. WHAT IF HE LET IT SLIP? THE KITS COULD GET HURT.

I...CAN'T TELL YOU EXACTLY WHAT HAPPENED.

BUT I KNOW YOU'RE MY FRIEND. I DON'T NEED ANY OTHER CAT.

FEATHERTAIL, THAT'S NO WAY TO LIVE.

WE NEED TO DEPEND ON OUR CLAN! THAT'S WHY WE HAVE CLANS!

I...

I JUST...

I'M SORRY.

I CAN'T.

WHATEVER.

THE TRUTH ABOUT SASHA AND TIGERSTAR JUST KEEPS WEIGHING HEAVIER AND HEAVIER ON ME.

ESPECIALLY NOW THAT HAWKPAW'S GETTING BIGGER. I DON'T KNOW IF I WOULD'VE NOTICED, IF I DIDN'T KNOW HIS SECRET...

...BUT HE'S STARTING TO LOOK A LOT LIKE HIS FATHER. AND HE MOVES THE SAME WAY. WITH THE SAME INTENSITY.

SO MUCH THAT IT'S... IT'S A LITTLE LIKE HAVING TIGERSTAR RIGHT BACK HERE IN THE CAMP.

SHOULD I TELL THE REST OF RIVERCLAN THE TRUTH?

BY KEEPING IT TO MYSELF, AM I PUTTING THE CLAN IN DANGER?

BUT I DON'T HAVE A CHOICE. I MADE A PROMISE.

EVEN THOUGH THE THOUGHT OF WHAT HAWKPAW MIGHT BECOME SENDS SHIVERS DOWN MY BACK.

OVER THE COURSE OF THIS GREENLEAF...

I'VE GOTTEN PRETTY GOOD AT KEEPING AN EYE ON THINGS.

AND I DON'T MISS IT WHEN LEOPARDSTAR AND SASHA HAVE A CONVERSATION ABOUT...

SOMETHING. SOMETHING UPSETTING.

NEXT TIME, SASHA.

YOU CAN BE SURE OF THAT.

HMMM.

CATS OF RIVERCLAN!

THE MOON HAS GROWN FULL — IT'S TIME FOR A GATHERING!

THESE CATS WILL ATTEND WITH ME:

STORMFUR. MISTYFOOT. MUDFUR. FEATHERTAIL...

INTERESTING. THE NAMES LEOPARDSTAR DOESN'T CALL, I THINK, ARE JUST AS IMPORTANT AS THE ONES SHE DOES.

BY THE TIME SHE FINISHES, I STILL HAVEN'T HEARD SASHA. OR HAWKPAW OR MOTHPAW.

IS SHE NOT YET READY FOR OTHER CLANS TO KNOW SHE'S TAKEN IN ROGUES?

OR IS IT SOMETHING ELSE?

SITE OF THE GATHERING.

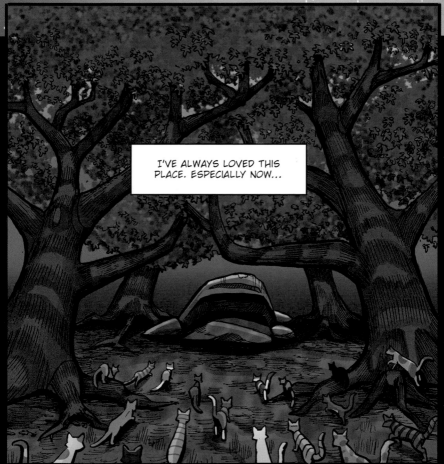

I'VE ALWAYS LOVED THIS PLACE. ESPECIALLY NOW...

...BECAUSE IT MEANS
I GET TO SEE MY FATHER.

CATS FROM ALL FOUR CLANS...

DIFFERENCES PUT ASIDE.
NO TERRITORIES TO FIGHT OVER.

PART OF ME WISHES WE
DIDN'T NEED CLANS AT ALL.

THEN IT WOULDN'T MATTER
HOW I FELT ABOUT RIVERCLAN.
OR ITS LEADER.

LEOPARDSTAR AND THEN THE OTHER CLAN LEADERS SHARE THEIR WORDS.

WHEN THEY ARE DONE, THE MOON HAS CROSSED THE SKY AND THE GATHERED WARRIORS ARE FREE TO CATCH UP WITH OTHER CLANS.

THE VOICES OF SO MANY SOCIALIZING CATS MINGLE INTO A KIND OF DULL ROAR.

I'M ONLY INTERESTED IN TALKING TO ONE, THOUGH.

FEATHERTAIL...STORMFUR... EACH TIME I SEE YOU, I CAN HARDLY BELIEVE IT.

MY KITS, FULL-GROWN WARRIORS.

I AM SO PROUD OF YOU TWO!

THANKS!

SO, HOW COME YOU'RE STILL REPRESENTING FIRESTAR? IS HE REALLY STILL SICK?

HE'S IMPROVING, DON'T WORRY.

I'M SURE HE'LL BE AT THE NEXT GATHERING.

HEY, THERE'S BRAMBLECLAW AND ASHFUR. LET ME GO CATCH UP WITH THEM.

FEATHERTAIL...YOU LOOK SAD. ARE YOU ALL RIGHT?

I'M FINE.

I NOTICED THAT YOU AND YOUR BROTHER WEREN'T EXACTLY MINGLING WITH THE REST OF YOUR CLANMATES.

ARE YOU SURE YOU'RE ALL RIGHT?

ARE YOU HAPPY IN RIVERCLAN? IS EVERY CAT TREATING YOU WELL THERE?

WELL...

NO CAT'S MISTREATING US, NO.

I JUST FIND IT HARD TO TRUST THE RIVERCLAN CATS.

AND ESPECIALLY LEOPARDSTAR.

AFTER EVERYTHING THAT HAPPENED.

I UNDERSTAND.

AND I WANT YOU TO REMEMBER...

YOU AND YOUR BROTHER ARE ALWAYS WELCOME IN THUNDERCLAN.

NO CAT WOULD OBJECT. YOU'RE MY KITS.

YOU HAVE THE RIGHT TO BECOME THUNDERCLAN WARRIORS IF THAT'S WHAT YOU WANT.

I DON'T KNOW.

STORMFUR DEFINITELY BELONGS IN RIVERCLAN. HE LOVES IT THERE.

AND IF HE'S HAPPY THERE, I'M HAPPY FOR HIM.

BUT I WOULD ALSO LOVE TO HAVE MY DAUGHTER IN THUNDERCLAN WITH ME.

I APPRECIATE THE OFFER. I MEAN IT.

BUT...AS LONG AS STORMFUR IS STILL PART OF RIVERCLAN...

I FEEL LIKE I SHOULD AT LEAST TRY TO FIND MY PLACE THERE, TOO.

ALL RIGHT.

BUT THE OFFER IS ALWAYS OPEN.

THANK YOU.

I SPEND THE NIGHT WITH MY FATHER'S WORDS ECHOING IN MY HEAD.

BUT THEN, THE NEXT MORNING, BEFORE I CAN GIVE THEM ANY FURTHER THOUGHT...

FEATHERTAIL. I NEED TO TALK TO YOU.

IN PRIVATE.

PLEASE.

WHAT DO YOU WANT, SASHA? I HAVE NOTHING TO SAY TO YOU.

MAYBE NOT, BUT I THINK YOU'LL WANT TO HEAR THIS.

I'M LEAVING RIVERCLAN.

SASHA, YOU...

YOU DON'T NEED TO LEAVE BECAUSE OF ME.

I DON'T LIKE WHAT YOU'VE DONE, BUT I PROMISED TO KEEP YOUR SECRET, AND I MEANT IT.

THIS ISN'T BECAUSE OF YOU.

LEOPARDSTAR WANTS ME TO JOIN THE CLAN. OFFICIALLY.

SHE ALREADY THINKS I'VE STALLED FOR TOO LONG.

SHE WANTS TO INTRODUCE US ALL TO THE OTHER CLANS.

IT'S GENEROUS. AND AMAZING. AND I CAN'T DO IT.

TOO MANY OF THE SHADOWCLAN CATS KNEW ME WHEN I WAS WITH TIGERSTAR...

...AND IF THEY SEE ME WITH MY KITS, THEY'LL KNOW TIGERSTAR WAS MOTH AND HAWK'S FATHER.

ESPECIALLY SINCE HAWK'S LOOKING MORE LIKE TIGERSTAR EVERY DAY.

THEY WON'T LET US STAY. NOT AFTER ALL THAT TIGERSTAR DID.

AT BEST, THEY'LL DRIVE US OUT.

AT WORST... THEY'LL KILL US.

I CAN'T ARGUE WITH HER. SHE'S RIGHT, AND WE BOTH KNOW IT.

SO I'M LEAVING.

HAWKPAW AND MOTHPAW HAVE DECIDED TO STAY HERE. I... URGED THEM TO. THEY ALREADY FEEL LIKE THEY BELONG HERE, AND...

THEY'LL BE SAFE THIS WAY.

WILL YOU STILL KEEP THEIR SECRET? EVEN AFTER I'M GONE?

PLEASE, FEATHERTAIL. PROMISE ME YOU WILL.

I ALREADY SAID I WOULD!

YOU THINK I'D PUT THOSE KITS IN DANGER JUST BECAUSE YOU'RE NOT HERE?

THIS IS THE LAST THING I'LL EVER ASK OF YOU. BUT I NEED TO KNOW.

WILL YOU PROMISE TO KEEP THEIR SECRET, FOREVER? NO MATTER WHAT? SAY IT. PLEASE SAY IT.

I WON'T TURN AGAINST YOUR KITS, SASHA. I WON'T DO WHAT TIGERSTAR DID.

I PROMISE.

I'VE SPENT ALL DAY NOW TRYING TO FIGURE OUT SOME WAY FOR SASHA TO STAY IN RIVERCLAN. TO STAY WITH HER KITS.

I COULDN'T COME UP WITH ANYTHING. SHE'S RIGHT.

IF HAWKPAW AND MOTHPAW ARE GOING TO STAY SAFE, SASHA CAN'T BE HERE ANYMORE.

I SHOULD BE GLAD TO SEE HER LEAVE.

BUT I'M NOT.

SHE WAS A GOOD FRIEND. FOR A WHILE.

EVEN IF IT WAS ALL BASED ON A LIE.

IT'S GETTING COLDER NOW.

SUITS ME FINE.

THE COLDER IT GETS, THE MORE IMPORTANT IT IS TO BRING BACK PREY.

AND AS LONG AS I'M OUT HERE, BRINGING BACK PREY...

NO CAT HAS ANY REASON TO BOTHER ME

I WAS RIGHT WHEN I TOLD GRAYSTRIPE THAT STORMFUR BELONGS HERE.

HE'S A RIVERCLAN CAT, THROUGH AND THROUGH. WHICH IS GREAT...

EXCEPT, THE MORE TIME HE SPENDS WITH ALL OF THEM, THE LESS TIME HE HAS FOR ME.

I MISS HIM.

BUT IT'S BETTER TO BE BY MYSELF.

NOT TO MENTION, BEING ALONE MAKES IT EASIER TO KEEP WATCH OVER HAWKPAW AND MOTHPAW.

AND YET...

THEY BOTH SEEM LIKE PRAISEWORTHY APPRENTICES. I NEVER SEE THEM ACTING LAZY OR STUBBORN.

THERE'S SOMETHING ABOUT HAWKPAW. I CAN'T SHAKE IT. SOMETHING ABOUT HIM THAT BOTHERS ME.

I TELL MYSELF IT'S "SOMETHING." THAT'S NOT HONEST. I KNOW EXACTLY WHAT IT IS.

DAY BY DAY, HAWKPAW GET FIERCER. MORE VICIOUS.

IS HE JUST A TALENTED FIGHTER?

OR IS HE ON HIS WAY TO BECOMING AS DANGEROUS AS HIS FATHER?

FVVERAIL!

FVVERAIL!

LOOK WHAT I CAUGHT! LOOK AT THE SIZE OF IT! HAVE YOU EVER SEEN A SQUIRREL THAT FAT BEFORE?

YEAH. VERY NICE.

I KNOW HAWKPAW AND MOTHPAW HAVE TO BE WONDERING WHY I DON'T LIKE THEM ANYMORE.

I MADE A PROMISE TO LOOK OUT FOR THEM. PROTECT THEM. KEEP THEIR SECRET.

BUT, STARCLAN HELP ME... I CAN'T TREAT THEM THE WAY I USED TO.

I JUST CAN'T.

BEFORE I KNOW IT, LEAF-BARE IS ON US.

AND IT'S A HARD ONE. PREY'S GETTING SCARCE...AND TEMPERS FLARE.

RIVERCLAN —
ATTACK!

I DON'T THINK LEOPARDSTAR
WAS EXPECTING HAWKPAW
TO CHARGE LIKE THAT...

...BUT IT ONLY TAKES A COUPLE OF
HEARTBEATS FOR THE WINDCLAN
PATROL TO DECIDE IT ISN'T WORTH IT.

HAWKPAW.

YOU DID WELL HERE. SOMETIMES A DROP OF INTIMIDATION IS WORTH A RIVER OF CLAWS AND FANGS.

BUT NEXT TIME, WAIT FOR MY SIGNAL BEFORE CHARGING HEADLONG INTO BATTLE.

UNDERSTOOD?

UNDERSTOOD. SORRY, LEOPARDSTAR.

LITTLE KILLER, YOU ARE!

"LITTLE KILLER," BLACKCLAW SAYS.

WHAT IF HE'S RIGHT?

I CAN'T STOP THINKING ABOUT IT.

CAN'T SHAKE THE SUSPICION.

WHAT IF HE DOES HAVE HIS FATHER'S INSTINCTS?

I HOPE I'M WRONG. I HOPE HAWKPAW AND MOTHPAW SIMPLY BECOME A COUPLE OF FINE RIVERCLAN WARRIORS.

I JUST WISH I COULD BE SURE OF THAT.

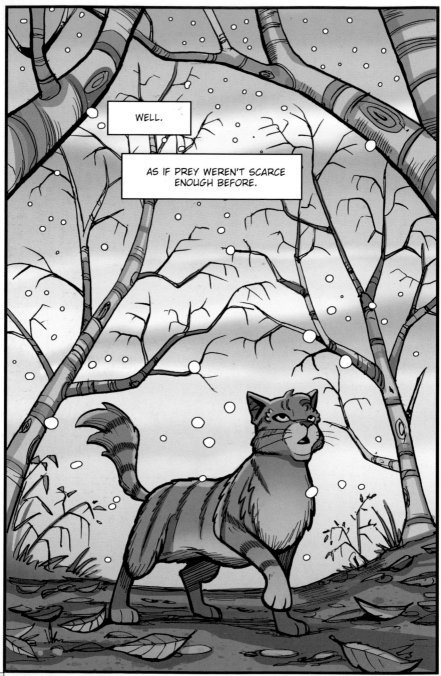

WELL.

AS IF PREY WEREN'T SCARCE ENOUGH BEFORE.

SOMETIMES I WISH WE COULD DO WHAT THE SQUIRRELS DO.

SNFF SNFF

LIVE OFF OF NUTS HIDDEN IN THE GROUND.

THE SQUIRRELS BARELY COME OUT AT ALL WHEN IT'S LIKE THIS.

HARDLY ANY PREY DOES.

I SUPPOSE IT'S ALWAYS BEEN LIKE THIS.

LEAF-BARE IS NEVER EASY.

BUT IT DOESN'T MAKE IT ANY LESS PAINFUL TO ENDURE.

WE USUALLY HAVE IT THE BEST OUT OF ANY OF THE CLANS. USUALLY THE FISH NEVER STOP SWIMMING...

NO MATTER HOW COLD IT GETS.

BUT IT DOESN'T MATTER HOW MANY FISH THERE ARE, IF YOU CAN'T GET TO THEM.

THAT WAS MOSSPELT!

SHE'S STANDING GUARD!

MOSSPELT? MOSSPELT!

I TRIED...COULDN'T...

COULDN'T STOP IT...

STARVATION IS LIKE A WOUND.

AND WOUNDED ANIMALS...

ARE THE MOST DANGEROUS.

WHAM!

YIPE!

SLLLPP

WHOMP!

IT'S DOWN! DIG IN, WARRIORS!

DRIVE THE BEAST OUT!

YIPE YIPE YIPE YIPE!

THE NEXT DAY, LEOPARDSTAR MAKES THE ANNOUNCEMENT THAT I KNEW WAS COMING.

LET ALL CATS OLD ENOUGH TO SWIM GATHER TO HEAR MY WORDS!

WE ARE NO LONGER SAFE. THAT FOX KNOWS WHERE WE ARE.

WITH THE RIVER FROZEN, WE DON'T HAVE ANY DEFENSES AGAINST IT COMING BACK.

IT MIGHT EVEN BRING OTHER FOXES.

LET IT COME!

WE BEAT IT ONCE! WE CAN DO IT AGAIN!

CATS AROUND HAWKPAW LAUGH...

...BUT LAUGHTER OR NOT, WE ALL KNOW WE MIGHT NOT BE SO LUCKY A SECOND TIME.

I WANT TO PUT TOGETHER A SMALL, QUICK-MOVING PATROL TO GO OUT AFTER THE FOX.

WE'LL TRACK IT TO ITS DEN AND THEN, WHEN WE KNOW WHERE IT LIVES, RETURN WITH A LARGER PATROL – INCLUDING WARRIORS FROM OTHER CLANS.

THEY'LL WANT TO GET RID OF THIS THREAT JUST AS MUCH AS WE DO.

WHO'S GOING TO BE ON THIS PATROL?

I'LL BE LEADING IT MYSELF.

AND I'LL TAKE WITH ME...

MY APPRENTICE.

HAWKPAW.

LEOPARDSTAR, HE'S NOT READY!

AN APPRENTICE DOESN'T BELONG ON SUCH A DANGEROUS MISSION!

HAWKPAW HAS ALREADY PROVEN THAT HE'S JUST AS IMPRESSIVE A FIGHTER AS WARRIORS MANY SEASONS HIS ELDER.

AND DON'T FORGET: I AM HIS MENTOR. I'LL PROTECT HIM.

IF HE NEEDS PROTECTING.

BECAUSE LEOPARDSTAR HAS A GREAT HISTORY OF KEEPING APPRENTICES SAFE.

OH, HUSH, WILL YOU?

MISGIVINGS OR NOT... TALENT AS A WARRIOR OR NOT...

I'M THE ONE WHO PROMISED THEIR MOTHER THAT I'D KEEP HAWKPAW AND MOTHPAW SAFE.

I SEE NO OTHER CHOICE.

LEOPARDSTAR!

I VOLUNTEER FOR THE PATROL WITH YOU AND HAWKPAW!

UM – YEAH! AND ME!

I VOLUNTEER! I WANT TO GO TOO!

WHAT'RE YOU DOING? THAT FOX ALMOST KILLED YOU! IT ALMOST KILLED ALL OF US.

FIRST, SO WHAT? THAT JUST MEANS WE OWE IT AN EXTRA BEATING.

SECOND, YOU'RE NOT ABOUT TO LEAVE ME BEHIND IF YOU'RE HEADING OFF INTO SOMETHING THIS DANGEROUS!

ALL RIGHT. HAWKPAW, FEATHERTAIL, STORMFUR, AND ME.

FOUR CATS ARE ENOUGH.

THE REST OF THE CLAN AGREES:

SINCE WE'RE GOING TO NEED OUR STRENGTH, THEY LET US HAVE WHAT LITTLE IS LEFT ON THE FRESH-KILL PILE.

AND OF COURSE OUR MEDICINE CAT BRINGS US SOME TRAVELING HERBS.

THE WHOLE CLAN IS THERE AS WE LEAVE, BUT NOT MANY OF THEM SAY ANYTHING.

I WOULDN'T KNOW WHAT TO SAY, EITHER. "GOOD LUCK?" "HAVE A SAFE TRIP?"..."DON'T GET KILLED?"

WHUGH!

WELL.

AT LEAST WE MADE IT THROUGH THE NIGHT.

WONDER IF THE FOX CAME AND CARRIED LEOPARDSTAR AWAY WHILE WE SLEPT?

AH. NO.

COULDN'T GET THAT LUCKY.

GOOD MORNING, FEATHERTAIL. I WAS FORTUNATE WITH THIS MORNING'S HUNT.

WANT TO SHARE IT WITH ME?

I CAN CATCH MY OWN PREY, THANKS.

OFFER TO SHARE PREY WITH ME.

AS IF SHE CARES ANYTHING ABOUT ME.

SHE MADE IT PLENTY CLEAR HOW SHE FEELS ABOUT ME...

AND ABOUT MY BROTHER.

I WANT NOTHING FROM HER.

WAIT — HOLD ON.

SNFF SNFF

IT'S THIS CURSED WIND.

I'VE LOST THE SCENT.

I DON'T KNOW ABOUT ANY OTHER CAT, BUT I THINK WE'VE COME ABOUT AS FAR AS WE CAN.

LET'S HEAD BACK TO CAMP. PICK THIS UP AGAIN WHEN WE CAN ALL FEEL OUR PAWS.

HEY! HEY!

IT'S ALL RIGHT! I'VE GOT THE SCENT!

STORMFUR'S RIGHT. WE'VE DONE WHAT WE CAME TO DO.

TIME TO GO AND GATHER UP THAT LARGER PATROL, ISN'T IT?

HAWKPAW!

GET YOUR TAIL BACK HERE!

I WANNA SEE WHAT'S INSIDE!

IT'S ALL RIGHT, LEOPARDSTAR!

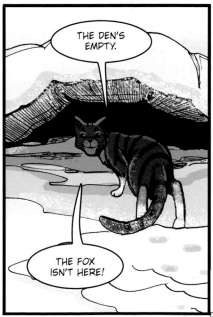

THE DEN'S EMPTY.

THE FOX ISN'T HERE!

GRRRRRHHH

GRRRRRHHH!

HAWKPAW! STAY BEHIND US!

FEATHERTAIL! STORMFUR! WE NEED TO GET THE FOX TO BACK OFF –

JUST FAR ENOUGH THAT WE CAN ALL MAKE A RUN FOR IT!

HIT IT HARD AND FAST! MAKE IT RETREAT, LIKE WE DID IN CAMP!

READY...

NOW!

AAIIIRRRHH!

WHAMM!

UNF!

ALL OF YOU –

RUN! RUN!

CAN'T YOU HEAR ME?

THIS IS... YOUR CHANCE!

LEAVE ME!

GO... PLEASE... GO!

ABRUPTLY IT FEELS LIKE THE WORLD HAS COME TO A STOP. LIKE A WHOLE SEASON PASSES BETWEEN EACH HEARTBEAT.

STARING INTO LEOPARDSTAR'S EYES...

SEEING THE PAIN, THE FEAR...

THE SACRIFICE.

NO MATTER WHAT SHE'S DONE IN THE PAST...

SHE'S WILLING TO GIVE UP ONE OF HER LIVES FOR MINE NOW.

AND I KNOW...

FEATHERTAIL!

YAAAOOOWR!

WHUMP

TAP
TAP

CAN YOU ALL... MAKE IT BACK... TO CAMP?

I CAN MAKE IT. STORMFUR?

I'M SURE AS STARCLAN NOT STAYING OUT HERE ANOTHER NIGHT.

WE'RE FINE, LEOPARDSTAR. LET'S GET YOU BACK TO MUDFUR.

FEATHERTAIL... YOU KNOW CLAN LEADERS HAVE...NINE LIVES... RIGHT?

YES. SO?

SO YOU SHOULD HAVE... DONE WHAT I SAID...AND LEFT ME THERE.

WELL.

THAT'S NOT WHAT CLANMATES DO.

HERE, LEAN AGAINST ME.

I'VE FELT PRIDE BEFORE. BUT IT'S ALWAYS BEEN IN SOMETHING I'VE DONE FOR MYSELF.

THIS FEELING... THIS PRIDE IN MY CLAN...

THAT'S NEW.

FEATHERTAIL. STORMFUR. I...

I NEED TO SAY SOMETHING TO YOU... TO YOU BOTH.

I'VE WANTED TO SAY THIS FOR A LONG TIME...

BUT I COULD NEVER FIND THE RIGHT MOMENT.

I AM SO SORRY FOR THE WAY I TREATED YOU. FOR ALLYING WITH TIGERSTAR. I WAS SO...

SO VERY WRONG.

I NEVER SHOULD'VE TRUSTED HIM.

AND I SHOULD'VE PROTECTED YOU.

MY OWN AMBITION BLINDED ME UNTIL IT WAS FAR TOO LATE. LISTEN, I...

I'M GRATEFUL YOU'VE BOTH RETURNED TO RIVERCLAN. AND I'LL UNDERSTAND IF YOU CAN NEVER FORGIVE ME.

BUT I WANT YOU TO KNOW...I'M SO PROUD OF THE WARRIORS YOU'VE GROWN INTO.

NO THANKS TO ME.

I'VE BEGUN TO FEEL THIS SENSATION. A LITTLE AT A TIME, HERE AND THERE.

TEACHING THE KITS TO SWIM. SPENDING TIME WITH SASHA.

LIKE TINY CRACKS IN THE ICE OF A FROZEN RIVER.

BUT NOW... HEARING LEOPARDSTAR'S WORDS, IT'S...

...IT'S AS IF THE RIVER ICE HAS BROKEN, ALL AT ONCE, AND IT'S ALMOST OVERWHELMING ME.

I'M NOT ANGRY ANYMORE.

LEOPARDSTAR, I – I THINK I CAN SPEAK FOR STORMFUR, TOO.

WE BOTH KNOW THINGS HAVE CHANGED IN RIVERCLAN.

AND WE FORGIVE YOU.

ABSOLUTELY.

THANK YOU.

THANK YOU BOTH.

I MAKE MYSELF A PROMISE, THERE ON THE SPOT. I'M GOING TO LET *GO* OF THE PAST.

LET MYSELF BECOME FULLY PART OF RIVERCLAN.

AND DEFEND AND PROTECT EVERY CAT IN IT.

DRIP
DRIP DRIP

CRUNCH

SWISH

RIVERCLAN ALSO MADE IT THROUGH LEAF-BARE WITHOUT LOSING ANY CATS...

...BUT IT WAS A VERY NEAR THING, AND WOULD HAVE BEEN DIFFERENT...

...HAD A RIVERCLAN PATROL NOT TRACKED AND KILLED A FOX THAT HAD ASSAULTED OUR CAMP.

THAT PATROL OWED A GREAT MEASURE OF ITS SUCCESS TO TWO WARRIORS IN PARTICULAR –

FEATHERTAIL AND STORMFUR.

WITHOUT THEIR BRAVERY, I WOULD NOT BE SPEAKING TO YOU TONIGHT.

NEWLEAF.

NEW BEGINNINGS.

I NEVER REALLY THOUGHT
I COULD HAVE A NEW BEGINNING.

NOT TILL NOW.

BUT I'M STARTING TO THINK MY LIFE...

...UP TO THIS POINT...

...WAS SORT OF LIKE A TREE.

I HAD TO LET ALL THE OLD LEAVES TURN YELLOW AND FALL OFF...

...BEFORE THE NEW, FRESH, GREEN ONES COULD GROW IN.

NEW BEGINNINGS INDEED.

IT FEELS GOOD TO BE PART OF A CLAN.

TO HAVE FRIENDS...

TIME TO STOP WATCHING MOTHPAW AND HAWKPAW SO CLOSELY, TOO.

I NEED TO JUDGE THEM AS THE CATS THEY ARE...

...AND NOT BY ANYTHING ELSE.

FRIENDS I CAN TRUST.

ESPECIALLY NOT BY WHO THEIR *FATHER* WAS.

DON'T MISS THIS WARRIORS
GRAPHIC NOVEL ADVENTURE

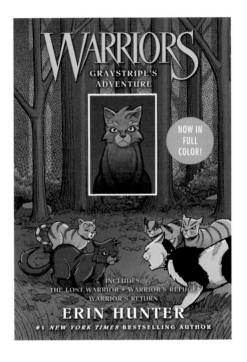

Keep reading for a sneak peek!

THIS IS MY FOREST. MY HOME.
IT USED TO BE BEAUTIFUL...

...BEFORE THE TWOLEGS CAME
AND STARTED RIPPING IT APART.

NOW THEY'RE TRYING TO CAPTURE
ALL OF THE CATS WHO LIVE HERE...
AND ONLY STARCLAN KNOWS WHAT
THEY'LL DO TO THEM.

SOME OF THESE CATS ARE ROGUES...

...BUT A LOT OF THEM BELONG TO THUNDERCLAN. MY CLAN.

MY NAME IS GRAYSTRIPE.

I'M A THUNDERCLAN WARRIOR.

AND I'LL DIE BEFORE I LET THESE CATS SUFFER ANY LONGER.

AOW!

THE PLAN'S WORKING SO FAR. I DISTRACT THE TWOLEGS...

...WHILE SQUIRRELPAW LEADS BRAMBLECLAW, RAINWHISKER, AND THORNCLAW INTO THE TWOLEGS' MONSTER.

GO! GO! GET OUT OF HERE!

WE'RE NOT LEAVING WITHOUT YOU, BRIGHTHEART!

ERIN HUNTER

is inspired by a fascination with the ferocity of the natural world. As well as having great respect for nature in all its forms, Erin enjoys creating rich, mythical explanations for animal behavior. She is also the author of the Survivors, Seekers, and Bravelands series.

Find out more online at www.warriorcats.com.

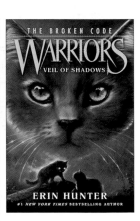

WARRIORS

How many have you read?

Dawn of the Clans
- ○ #1: The Sun Trail
- ○ #2: Thunder Rising
- ○ #3: The First Battle
- ○ #4: The Blazing Star
- ○ #5: A Forest Divided
- ○ #6: Path of Stars

Power of Three
- ○ #1: The Sight
- ○ #2: Dark River
- ○ #3: Outcast
- ○ #4: Eclipse
- ○ #5: Long Shadows
- ○ #6: Sunrise

The Prophecies Begin
- ○ #1: Into the Wild
- ○ #2: Fire and Ice
- ○ #3: Forest of Secrets
- ○ #4: Rising Storm
- ○ #5: A Dangerous Path
- ○ #6: The Darkest Hour

Omen of the Stars
- ○ #1: The Fourth Apprentice
- ○ #2: Fading Echoes
- ○ #3: Night Whispers
- ○ #4: Sign of the Moon
- ○ #5: The Forgotten Warrior
- ○ #6: The Last Hope

The New Prophecy
- ○ #1: Midnight
- ○ #2: Moonrise
- ○ #3: Dawn
- ○ #4: Starlight
- ○ #5: Twilight
- ○ #6: Sunset

A Vision of Shadows
- ○ #1: The Apprentice's Quest
- ○ #2: Thunder and Shadow
- ○ #3: Shattered Sky
- ○ #4: Darkest Night
- ○ #5: River of Fire
- ○ #6: The Raging Storm

Select titles also available as audiobooks!

HARPER
An Imprint of HarperCollinsPublishers

www.warriorcats.com • www.shelfstuff.com

SUPER EDITIONS

GUIDES

FULL-COLOR GRAPHIC NOVELS

EBOOKS AND NOVELLAS

HARPER
An Imprint of HarperCollinsPublishers

www.warriorcats.com • www.shelfstuff.com

Don't miss these other Erin Hunter series!

SURVIVORS

Survivors
- ◯ #1: The Empty City
- ◯ #2: A Hidden Enemy
- ◯ #3: Darkness Falls
- ◯ #4: The Broken Path
- ◯ #5: The Endless Lake
- ◯ #6: Storm of Dogs

Survivors: The Gathering Darkness
- ◯ #1: A Pack Divided
- ◯ #2: Dead of Night
- ◯ #3: Into the Shadows
- ◯ #4: Red Moon Rising
- ◯ #5: The Exile's Journey
- ◯ #6: The Final Battle

SEEKERS

Seekers
- ◯ #1: The Quest Begins
- ◯ #2: Great Bear Lake
- ◯ #3: Smoke Mountain
- ◯ #4: The Last Wilderness
- ◯ #5: Fire in the Sky
- ◯ #6: Spirits in the Stars

Seekers: Return to the Wild
- ◯ #1: Island of Shadows
- ◯ #2: The Melting Sea
- ◯ #3: River of Lost Bears
- ◯ #4: Forest of Wolves
- ◯ #5: The Burning Horizon
- ◯ #6: The Longest Day

HARPER
An Imprint of HarperCollinsPublishers

www.shelfstuff.com

www.warriorcats.com/survivors • www.warriorcats.com/seekers